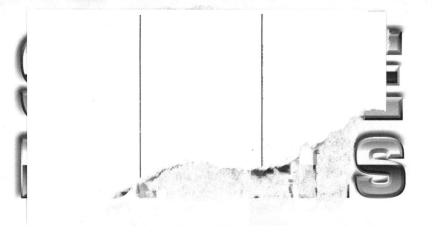

SILENCE ON SATURN

On loan from

**SCHOOL
LIBRARIES**
RESOURCES
SERVICE

Telephone: 020 8359 3931
Fax: 020 8201 3018
E-mail: slrs@barnet.gov.uk

NASEN House, 4/5 Amber Business Village, Amber Close, Amington,
Tamworth, Staffordshire, B77 4RP

Rising Stars UK Ltd.
7 Hatchers Mews, Bermondsey Street, London SE1 3GS
www.risingstars-uk.com

Text © Tommy Donbavand 2014
Design and layout © Rising Stars UK Ltd. 2014
The right of Tommy Donbavand to be identified as the author of this work
has been asserted by him in accordance with the Copyright, Design and
Patents Act, 1998.

Published 2014

Author: Tommy Donbavand
Cover design: Sarah Garbett @ Sg Creative Services
Illustrations: Alan Brown for Advocate Art
Text design and typesetting: Sarah Garbett @ Sg Creative Services
Publisher: Fiona Lazenby
Editorial consultants: Jane Friswell and Dee Reid
Editorial: Fiona Tomlinson and Sarah Chappelow

MIX
Paper from
responsible sources
FSC
www.fsc.org   FSC® C011748

CONTENTS

DAN

Name: Dan Fireball
Rank: Captain
Age: 12
Home planet: Earth
Most likely to: hide behind the Captain's chair and ask timidly, "Are we there yet?"

ASTRA

Name: Astra Moon
Rank: Second Officer
Age: 11
Home planet: The Moon
Most likely to: face up to The Geezer, strike a karate pose and say, "Bring it on!"

HS INFINITY

THE GEEZER

Name: Volt
Rank: Agent
Age: Really old!
Home planet: Venus
Most likely to: puff steam from his shoulder exhausts and announce, "Hop completed!"

Name: Gus Buster
Rank: Head of COSMIC
Age: 15
Home planet: Earth
Most likely to: suddenly appear on the view screen and yell, "Fireball, where are you?"

COSMIC TRAINING SESSION
HISTORY OF THE SOLAR SYSTEM

VOLT

Greetings new recruits!

My name is Volt and I shall be your cyber-teacher for today.

You should read this section because if you wish to become **COSMIC** agents you must know the history of the Solar System.

Long ago, adults used to be in charge of everything. They had jobs, ran governments and were in charge of television remote controls.

Children were forced to stay in school until the age of 18. They had to do everything their parents told them. They were only given small amounts of currency, known as "pocket money".

There were lots of problems. Adults polluted the Earth and then went on to do the same – or even worse – on the remaining eight planets of our Solar System. In fact, for a long time, adults even refused to call Pluto a real planet!

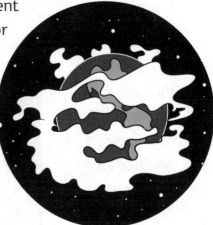

So, in the year 2281, the children took over.

Adults were made to retire at the age of 18

and were sent to retirement homes on satellites in space. Children just needed three years at school, so most children were working by the time they were eight years old.

The Solar System quickly became a much happier, safer and cleaner place to live.

However, not all of the adults liked having to retire at the age of 18. Some of them rebelled and escaped from their retirement homes on satellites in space. They began to cause trouble and commit crimes.

That's why **COSMIC** 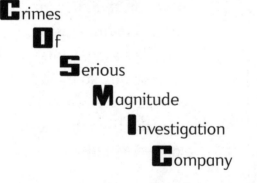 was created:

Crimes

   Of

      Serious

         Magnitude

           Investigation

              Company

The worst of these villains was known as The Geezer. The purpose of COSMIC was to stop The Geezer from committing crimes.

Members of COSMIC flew around the Solar System solving mysteries and bringing badly behaved adults to justice. The COSMIC spaceships could navigate an invisible series of magnetic tunnels called the Hop Field, so they were called Space Hoppers.

I myself, was a member of one such team of Space Hoppers, alongside the famous agents - Dan Fireball and Astra Moon.

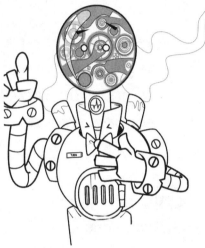

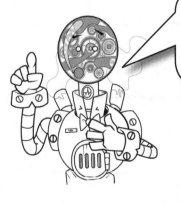

If you turn the page, you can read about one of the most exciting – yet quietest – missions we ever undertook ...

CHAPTER 1

THE STARS ARE OUT

HS INFINITY DATA LOG
MISSION REPORT 2:
SILENCE ON SATURN
REPORT BEGINS ...

Second Officer Astra Moon stepped onto the command deck of the HS Infinity, tapping at the keyboard of her handheld computer.

"Volt has almost finishing upgrading the ship's flight systems, Captain," she said.

"Excellent," replied Captain Dan Fireball from his command chair at the front of the spaceship.

He didn't look up from the screen of his tablet computer. "When he's finished that, tell him to get started on upgrading the ship's flight systems."

"You're not listening to me again, Dan!" Astra snapped. "I said Volt's almost finished."

Dan spun around in his chair, "Did you say 'Volt's always fishing?'"

Astra sighed. "A good COSMIC captain should listen to his crew," she grumbled.

"I'm great at listening!" protested Dan.

"You switch your ears off whenever you've got your head stuck in your computer," said Astra. "What game are you playing this time? Angry Asteroids?"

Dan covered the screen of his tablet with his hand. "I'm not playing a game," he said, "I'm … studying the stars."

"Oh, sorry!" said Astra. "Which stars are you studying at the moment?"

Dan blushed. "I'm … er … not exactly sure what they're called."

"Well, let's see …" said Astra, tapping a command into her keyboard. "I can easily transfer the video feed from your tablet to the ship's view screen."

"No!" cried Dan, but it was too late. The huge screen at the front of the ship hissed, and then began to show footage from outside a glitzy cinema. A TV presenter with a huge, wobbling quiff of hair was standing on a red carpet, interviewing celebrities as they arrived for a lavish awards ceremony.

"This is Zane Sparkle, live for Holograph TV at this year's Ringie Awards! Just about every big name in the Solar System is here tonight, hoping that they will be leaving with one of the movie industry's top prizes!"

Astra folded her arms. "Studying the stars, Dan?"

"Well, they are stars!" Dan insisted. "Movie stars! And look – there's my favourite – Silly Crystal!"

On the screen, crowds cheered as a large alien made entirely out of shimmering diamond swaggered into view. Zane Sparkle spotted the star and hurried over to hold a microphone up to the actor's face.

"And here I am with Silly Crystal!" said Zane Sparkle on the screen. "He's favourite to win the Ringie Award for 'Best See-Through Actor in a Comedy Film' tonight. Silly, can you tell us about your new movie?"

Silly Crystal removed his stylish sunglasses and winked at the camera. With a cheeky smile, he opened his mouth to reply — but nothing came out.

He just grabbed at his throat and made a tiny croaking noise.

"Silly? Are you okay?" asked Zane. Then the TV presenter clutched at his own throat. "Oh no ... something's wro—." He continued to move his lips, but no sound came out.

Dan and Astra watched in horror as, one by one, the movie stars all grabbed at their throats and fell silent. Within seconds, everyone on screen was panicking and calling for help – but nobody made a sound.

"Is it a problem with the screen?" asked Astra, turning up the volume. It didn't help.

"I don't think so," said Dan. "Someone has attacked the stars at the Ringie Awards on Saturn." He grabbed the remote control from Astra and hit the pause button. "And I know just who's responsible."

He stepped up to the screen and pointed to a figure standing among the crowds of movie fans and autograph hunters. It was an adult dressed in a grey cardigan, and he was grinning wickedly.

Astra gasped as she recognised the figure. "The Geezer!" she exclaimed.

CHAPTER 2

EYES ON THE PRIZE

Volt, an old-fashioned brass robot, rolled onto the command deck on his single wheel, steam pumping from the twin exhaust pipes rising up from his shoulders. He stopped next to a computer screen and began to wave his arms around in the air.

"Has your gyroscope gone wonky again?" Dan asked.

"No, Master Dan," Volt replied. "Now that I have finished working with the flight systems, I am bringing the command deck's computers up to date."

"It looks like you're conducting an orchestra." said Dan.

"In many ways I am, Sir," said Volt. "Take a look through the lens of your tablet at the air around us. I recommend magnification level seven."

Dan held up his computer tablet and clicked on the zoom button. Suddenly, he could see that the air was buzzing with millions of tiny, golden dots. "What are they?" he asked.

"These are nanobots," Volt replied. "Tiny robots which can fly inside the controls of the HS Infinity to repair or upgrade the computer systems. I am currently signalling instructions to them."

Dan waved his hand through the air, forcing a cloud of the tiny androids to dash out of the way. "They're so small!"

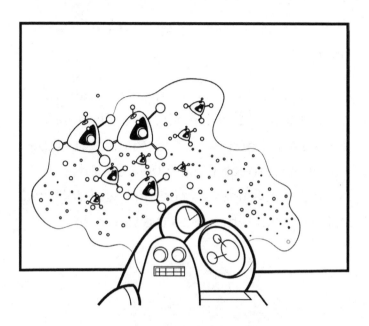

"Size really isn't important Master Dan," said Volt. "Each of these microscopic androids has at least as much processing power as I do, some even more."

"And they take up a lot less space!" said Dan, winking to Astra. "Maybe you could retire along with the adults, and we'll get a few thousand of these things instead."

Volt froze, his arms finally still. "But I have served your family for generations, sir!" Steam blasted from both of his exhaust pipes.

"Don't panic Volt," laughed Astra. "Dan is only joking."

"Ah, yes," said Volt quietly. "Humour. Very good, Master Dan. Ha. Ha. Ha." The robot turned away and went back to conducting the nanobots through their duties. "Sounds like someone else finds you as funny as I do!" said Astra as Dan returned to the view screen.

"I don't need to be funny," said Dan. "Not when there are great comedians like Silly Crystal out there."

"He'll have to start doing silent comedies if we can't work out what The Geezer is up to and put a stop to it," said Astra. "Now, sit down."

"Why?" said Dan. "I can captain this ship standing up if I like."

"Suit yourself," said Astra. "It's just that we're about to enter the Hop Field." She slammed her palm down onto a large yellow button on her desk.

HS Infinity leapt sideways into one of the invisible magnetic tunnels that make up the Hop Field, connecting every planet and moon in the Solar System. Within moments, the ship was whizzing along.

For a few seconds everything went fuzzy —
as though the entire universe was made out
of candy floss. Astra clung on to the edge of
her desk. Her mouth was dry, and it felt like
someone was tickling her all over.

Then, everything snapped back into place,
causing Volt to roll backwards away from his
own desk, and sending Dan sprawling to
the floor.

"I warned you!" said Astra with a smile as
Dan pulled himself up into his chair.

The still-silent celebrities vanished from the
view screen and, a few seconds later, were
replaced with the image of a vast, pale blue
planet surrounded by silver rings.

"Hop completed," said Volt. "The HS
Infinity has arrived at Saturn."

Dan grinned. "The Hollywood of the
Solar System!"

"Hollywood?" said Astra. "Where's that?"

"It's where they made movies on Earth, in the old days," Dan explained. "They were usually only 2D back then – and you couldn't smell what was happening on screen – but some of those ancient films are classics now."

"And I suppose the actors still hoped to win ridiculous awards like The Ringies every year," added Astra.

"Awards aren't ridiculous," said Dan. "They're a way of recognising all the hard work and dedication these people put into their careers."

"I work hard, but nobody gives me awards." Astra pointed out.

"We can do the next best thing," said Dan. "Let's pretend there's a Best Space Hopper Award. Whichever one of us solves this mystery and returns Silly Crystal's voice, wins it!"

"You're on!" said Astra, shaking Dan's hand. "But I don't want you sulking for the rest of the week when I win."

"I don't sulk!" said Dan. "And I certainly won't this time, because I'm going to be the one to stop The Geezer and win the award!"

"We'll see," said Astra with a smile. "Right, buckle up — I'm taking the ship down to the surface. May the best Space Hopper win!"

CHAPTER 3

SILENCE IS GOLDEN

A stra landed the HS Infinity in front of the Titan Cinema in the middle of Saturn's largest city. She and Dan slipped on their helmets then, with Volt, they stepped out of the ship and onto the red carpet.

The crowds were still gathered outside the cinema, and they were all screaming and shouting but making no noise at all.

"This is creepy," said Astra as they made their way to the cinema entrance. "It's like someone has turned the volume all the way down."

"I always wanted to walk along a red carpet in front of adoring fans," said Dan. "I just didn't think it would happen like this."

Suddenly, someone grabbed hold of Dan's arm and spun him around. Dan found himself faced with a boy in his late teens, dressed in a glittering silver suit. It was the TV presenter, Zane Sparkle.

"Help me!" Zane mouthed. "I can't talk!"

"It's okay," said Dan as he ducked to avoid being hit by Zane's wobbling quiff of hair. "We're going to find out what's happened and fix it."

"Where is everyone?" asked Astra. "The carpet was full of celebrities when we saw it on the TV earlier."

Zane pointed to the cinema entrance. "All inside!" he said silently.

Dan, Astra and Volt hurried up the steps and ran into the cinema's main screening area. Dan froze, causing Astra and Volt to crash into him.

"What are you doing?" demanded Astra.

Dan stared around the room, open-mouthed. "Look at all the stars!" he gasped.

The cinema was packed full of actors, directors and producers – all rubbing at their throats and begging each other for help in silent panic.

"We'd better start looking for clues," suggested Astra. "Volt, start scanning and see if you can find out what caused this."

"Certainly, Miss Astra," said the robot, wheeling away.

Astra turned back to Dan. "Where do you want to start?"

But Dan wasn't listening. He was too busy star spotting. "Look — there's Dark Brooding, the Venusian guy who plays the pirate captain in all those action movies. And that's Scarlett Beauty — the prettiest actress in the entire Solar System!"

"She's a shape-shifter from Jupiter," said Astra. "Anyone can be beautiful if they can change shape to look however they choose!"

Dan ignored Astra's comment and continued spotting movie stars. "That's Glinty Teeth … and Skinny Diet … and Smug Chancer!" He patted the pockets of his COSMIC spacesuit. "Oh, I wish I'd brought my autograph book with me!"

"We can collect signatures after we've helped these people to talk again," said Astra. "So, I'll ask you one more time, where do you want to start looking for clues?"

This time Dan didn't reply. He stood, rooted to the spot with an expression of pure joy painted over his face. Silly Crystal was striding towards him. The diamond actor began to make shapes with his hands.

"I've no idea what he's doing — but it's brilliant!" said Dan with a sigh.

"It's sign language!" cried Astra. "I learned this back at home on the Moon." She watched as Silly made the shapes again.

"He wants to know who we are, and if we can help him," Astra explained.

Dan's eyes grew wide with excitement. "Silly Crystal wants to know my name!" he gushed. "Tell him I'm Captain Fireball from COSMIC, and that I'm his biggest fan!"

"I don't need to," said Astra. "You just did."

"What?" asked Dan, puzzled.

"He's not deaf, Dan!" said Astra. "He just can't talk!"

"Oh, yeah ..." said Dan, catching on at last. He spun back to face Silly Crystal, grinning as he spotted himself in hundreds of tiny reflections all over the actor's body. "We know who's done this to you," he said. "We just have to find him, and ... '

Dan's voice trailed away.

"What's wrong?" said Astra. "Don't tell me you've lost the ability to speak as well?"

Dan shook his head. "No," he hissed. "Look ..." He pointed to his reflection in Silly Crystal's diamond skin. Astra leaned in to get a better look. There, reflected in the background, she saw the image of a tall, thin man in a grey cardigan and slippers.

"The Geezer!" she whispered. "He's behind us!"

Dan nodded. "It doesn't look like he's noticed we're here," he said as quietly as possible. "We'll spin round on the count of three. One ... Two ... Three!"

Dan and Astra turned and reached out for The Geezer, each of them grabbing one of his arms.

"You're under arrest!" said Dan, proudly, producing a pair of handcuffs. "You have the right to remain silent — but these people don't. What have you done to them?"

"Done to them, sweetie?" said The Geezer with a smile. "Why, I haven't done anything to them at all!" Then, without warning, The Geezer's body began to ripple and squirm like goo.

"What's going on?" cried Dan, trying to maintain his grip on The Geezer's arm.

"He … he's changing somehow!" yelled Astra.

As quickly as it had started, the rippling stopped. Dan and Astra stared at their prisoner. It was no longer an older man dressed in grey, but a tall, beautiful alien with flowing red hair and pale green skin.

"Scarlett Beauty!" said Astra. "I told you she was a shape-shifter!"

"But why did she change to look like The Geezer?" asked Dan.

"And why is she the only one who can talk?" added Astra.

"He promised to give me my voice back if I pretended to be him," said Scarlett Beauty. "That's all, I promise. I have nothing to do with what has happened here."

"Really?" said Dan with a snarl. "Then where is The Geezer. The *real* one?"

"Why, I'm right behind you Dan Fireball," boomed a voice.

SMALL TALK

Ian spun round to see The Geezer on stage, stepping up to the microphone. He was clutching what appeared to be statues of the planet Saturn.

"The Ringie Awards!" gasped Dan. "He's stolen them!"

"And I'll steal a lot more before the day is out!" said The Geezer. Then, speaking into the microphone he announced, "Greetings to the great and good of the movie world. I am known as The Geezer and I have taken your voices!"

The room filled with shaking fists and silent threats.

"If you want them back, then all you have to do is hand over your money, credit cards and jewellery," continued The Geezer. "If you give me enough within ten minutes I will return your voices to you. If not, then you shall remain speechless, and the Solar System will have to get used to silent movies."

"Not if I've got anything to do with it," shouted Dan. He took a step forward, but Astra stopped him. "Look!" she exclaimed.

Dozens of other adults appeared around the room. They took up positions near the exits and blocked the way to the stage.

"The Geezer's henchmen," said Astra. "They'll be on top of you before you get anywhere near the stage."

"What should we do?" asked Dan, as The Geezer laughed wickedly.

Astra sighed. "I don't think there's anything we can do," she said. All around them, the movie stars began to empty their pockets and unfasten their necklaces. With silent groans of despair, they handed their valuables over to The Geezer's gang.

"Actually, there is one thing you can do, Master Dan," said a voice, accompanied by a burst of steam.

"Volt!" cried Astra. "What have you found out?"

"The problem appears to be nanobots, Miss Astra," the robot replied.

"You mean like those you used on the ship?" said Dan.

"Indeed," said Volt. "Only, these ones have entered the mouths of the guests, and have taken control of their vocal chords."

"So, that's what's keeping everyone silent." said Astra.

"Well," said Dan to Volt. "What are you waiting for? Wave your arms around and command them all to get out!"

"I'm afraid that isn't possible," said Volt. "These particular nanobots have been programmed to respond only to figures of authority. They would simply ignore an old robot like me."

Dan sighed. "Then we're stuck," he groaned. "Where's an authority figure when you need one?"

Astra shook her head slowly. "If only there was a Captain of a COSMIC Hop Ship here …" she said. Then she stared at Dan.

"Hang on!" cried Dan, his eyes sparkling.

"I'm the Captain of a COSMIC Hop Ship! I'm a figure of authority!"

Astra grinned. "The penny drops!"

"Okay," beamed Dan, rubbing his hands together. "What do I have to do?"

"The same as I was doing earlier, Master Dan," said Volt. "You have to conduct the nanobots with arm movements, and order them to leave the celebrities' throats."

"Shouldn't be a problem!" said Dan, cracking his knuckles. "How's this …?"

Dan stepped up to Silly Crystal, who opened his mouth wide. Astra and Volt watched as Dan began to wave his arms around in the air.

"He looks like an enthusiastic windmill," laughed Astra.

Suddenly, Silly Crystal clamped a hand over his nose and staggered backwards. Dan looked around in shock. All of the other celebrities were gripping their noses as well.

"What did I do wrong?" Dan asked Volt.

"It appears you have instructed everyone in the room to shoot bogies out of their noses," said Volt. "You need to be more gentle with your movements."

Dan slowed down his arm waving and swung slowly from side to side. He gestured with his fingers for the nanobots to leave the celebrities.

Astra held up her handheld computer and increased the magnification. "It's working!" she cried. On the screen, swarms of golden dots were streaming out of the movie stars' mouths. They gathered together in the air for a second then disappeared.

"I can talk!" croaked Smug Chancer, his throat finally free of nanobots.

"My voice is back!" said Dark Brooding.

"I can speak again!" exclaimed Skinny Diet.

"You did it!" cried Astra, throwing her arms around Dan's neck.

Dan stood back. "This mission isn't over yet," he said. "Look!" Dan pointed to where The Geezer was standing by the microphone. Dan marched up on to the stage, pushing his way past The Geezer's helpless henchmen.

"Okay, you're under arrest Geezer," said Dan, his voice amplified by the microphone. "COSMIC has the upper hand."

The Geezer pouted. "Do you really think so, sweetie?"

Dan froze. "That's not The Geezer!" he said to Astra. "That's Scarlett Beauty shape-shifting again!" He turned and raced back down the steps …

… only to stop right in front of an actress with pale green skin and bright red hair.

"But you're Scarlett Beauty," said Astra.

"Of course I am!" said the actress.

Dan sighed. "Then that means the person on the stage really was … '

" … The Geezer," finished Astra.

She and Dan dashed back to the stage. It was empty.

The sound of a spaceship blasting off echoed through the hall.

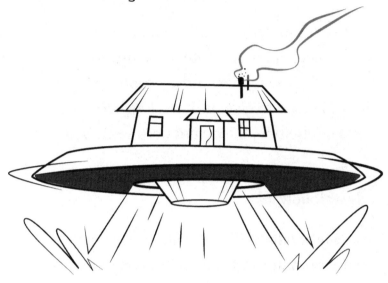

"And we let him go," sighed Dan.

"It seems that way," said Astra with a grim smile.

"But we can still give one award," said Silly Crystal as he strode over to Dan and Astra, his voice finally restored. He was clutching a statue of the planet Saturn. "The Geezer took all the Ringie Awards except one. And that award should be given to a Space Hopper!"

"Let it be me!" whispered Dan, crossing his fingers tightly.

Crystal smiled, revealing two rows of glistening, diamond teeth. "The award goes to the Space Hopper whose actions have most helped to give us our voices back. Ladies and gentlemen, the award goes to... Volt!"

The entire room began to clap and cheer loudly.

"My goodness!" said Volt, his exhaust pipes erupting with steam. "This is most unexpected!"

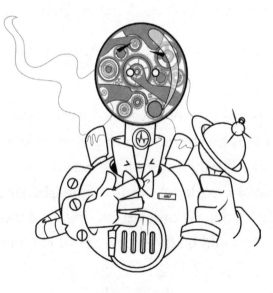

"It certainly is!" said Dan, slumping into one of the cinema's seats.

"Now, now!" said Astra, sitting beside him. "You promised you weren't going to sulk if you didn't win."

"I'm not sulking!" said Dan. "I'm just … speechless!"

THE END

Now read *Undead on Uranus* to find out what The Geezer gets up to next!

GLOSSARY

amplified – made louder

androids – robots or machines that look or behave a bit like a humans

asteroids – small, rocky planets that go round the Sun

ceremony – a formal occasion to celebrate something

gyroscope – a device, a bit like a spinning top, that is used to keep things balanced and level

henchmen – loyal helpers, who are usually up to no good

magnification – a way of making something look bigger

microscopic – too small to be seen with the eye

orchestra – a large group of musicians playing lots of different instruments all together

Venusian – a creature from the planet Venus

QUIZ QUESTIONS

1   What is the name of Dan's favourite movie star?

2   Who in the crowd at the Ringie Awards do Dan and Astra think has caused the attack?

3   What is Zane Sparkle's job?

4   What is Volt signaling to bring the command deck's computers up to date?

5   What is the reward for winning the competition between Dan and Astra?

6   Where does Scarlett Beauty come from?

7   Why did Scarlett Beauty pretend to be The Geezer?

8   Why can't Dan rush up on to the stage and arrest The Geezer?

9   What is keeping the guests silent?

10 How did The Geezer get away?

ABOUT THE AUTHOR

Tommy Donbavand writes full-time and lives in Lancashire with his family. He is also the author of the 13-book *Scream Street* series (currently in production for TV) and has written numerous books for children and young adults.

For Tommy, the best thing about being an author is getting to spend his days making up adventures for his readers. He also writes for 'The Bash Street Kids' in *The Beano*, which excites him beyond belief!

Find out more about Tommy and his other books at www.tommydonbavand.com

QUIZ ANSWERS

1. Silly Crystal
2. The Geezer
3. TV presenter
4. Nanobots
5. Being awarded the title of "Best Space Hopper".
6. Jupiter
7. Because he promised to give her voice back.
8. Because the Geezer's henchmen are blocking the way.
9. Nanobots
10. By pretending to be Scarlett Beauty.